D.O.C LOVE ©

C.L HAWKINS

DEDICATION

Father God, I thank you for giving me this gift. The gift of being creative and to be able to express myself through my writing. I am so blessed that you have given me the courage to show the world my talent. I would like to take this time to say that my short erotica stories were supposed to be my first book. Instead I decided to push it back and revamp some things. I just want to give you something that will have your imagination going. I hope that you enjoy.

I would like to thank everyone who supported me and pushed me to write. Especially the ones that stayed on my ass night and day: Emanuelle, Author C. Wilson (My Cee Cee), Nicky Bonds, Lovely, Chinese Nicky, Sino, Face, Marsha, Monique, AJ Writer, and Chantel. That's just naming a few. But there are a host of you that pushed me as well. I would like to say thank you to my Mr. Jay Dee. I don't know where to begin with you. Even in your absence you're still the hardest working man in this crew. You always try to push me beyond my means. You encourage me on days when I'm feeling depressed. Those are the days when I think that I don't have support, you prove me wrong. I truly am thankful for that. I'm not going to get mushy lol. You know what it is.

To my parents and my brothers, thank you for sticking by my side through everything.

Nah, I really must shout out my old Skyline Crew: Chanine, Tiesha, Melvina, Taka, Nicole, August, (My Poetry Crew.) Finally, my babies Queen Tya and My Campaign Manager (LOL) Demi-Aubrey. I do this for you. It's never too late to live out your dreams. I love you two to death.

With Love,

C.L HAWKINS

INTRO

You had a long day at work. All you want to do is go home, take a nice hot shower, pour yourself a glass of your favorite drink, and watch a movie. Or maybe you want to turn on the radio and listen to some Usher while you're lying next to your love. You're ready to prepare yourself for that massage, those long kisses and that essential foreplay. But when you get home reality hits you. You walk into an empty house. Not the scent of his or her cologne or perfume. There's no meal on the stove. You run and take a quick shower, because it's almost 8:30pm. This is your favorite time of the evening. You oil up your skin, pour you a drink and lay across your bed with only a robe on. You press play on the DVD player and mute on the remote control so no one can hear the moans from the television. Suddenly, the phone rings...

RING, RING, RING...

COLLECT CALL

"This is Green's Correctional Facility. You have a prepaid call from Travis. To accept the charges, press one... Thank you for using Securus, you may start your conversation."

"Hi Baby," Samantha screamed in the phone.

"What's up Babe." Travis replied.

Travis had been incarcerated for a year and a half. He has a year left. For him, every day seems like it's getting harder to be away from his girl. The thought of her always made him horny.

"What are you doing baby?" Travis asked.

"Just got out the shower. I'm rubbing some Baby Oil on my skin."

Travis' penis became hard just by hearing that.

"Oh yeah? Where your rubbing at?" he asked.

"Well, my thighs right now."

Samantha put more oil in her hands. She put the phone on speaker so that she could use both of her hands.

"Baby, you got my dick hard. Tell me what you're doing now," Travis asked eagerly.

Samantha smiled as she took off her robe. She then laid back onto the bed and opened her legs wide. She put baby oil all over her stomach and legs.

"Well, I'm rubbing this oil on my breast. These nipples are so hard."

She began to moan in between deep breaths.

"Now I'm rubbing on this clit."

She began to rub on it real slow. She closed her eyes and an image of Travis appeared; she missed him so much. Samantha's moans were getting loud.

"Baby tell me what you're doing. You're turning me on," Travis whispered into the phone.

"Travis" Samantha moaned, "this pussy is so wet."

"Really? Let me hear baby." Travis begged.

Samantha picked up the phone and placed it by her wet pussy. She began to play with herself. She put two fingers inside pushing them in and out slowly. Her moans were getting louder and louder. Samantha's pussy was so wet. It sounded like someone was stirring a pot of Mac and Cheese. This was driving Travis crazy. He pulled his dick out and began to jerk-off.

"How does it feel, babe?" he asked.

"It feels so good" she whispered.

Samantha looked over at the T.V and started to watch the porn that she had put on earlier. This was making her hornier.

"Pinch those nipples babe, tell me how it feels." Travis commanded.

Samantha moaned louder.

"Travis it feels so good. I miss you baby."

She quickly became emotional.

"Miss you too Sam. Keep playing with that pussy"

Samantha began to rub on her clit faster. Her moans and cries were out of control. Travis' dick was so hard that it was hurting him.

"YES Baby, cum for me, let me hear you." Travis begged.

"Baby, I wish you can watch me." Sam said.

"Trust me baby I can see your sexy body"

"You have sixty seconds remaining."

"Baby please let me hear you cum" Travis said in a rush.

Their time together on the phone was now on a countdown according to the operator. Samantha started moaning and moving her fingers back and forth. She kept her eyes closed, so that she could see Travis' face.

"Baby I'm about to cum" she screamed.

Travis got excited and started jerking even faster.

"Sam cum with me baby"

The sound of Travis' voice made her more wet.

"You have thirty seconds remaining."

Samantha felt all her juices pushing out.

"I'M CUMMIN BABE," she let out a big scream.

Travis exploded. "Samantha," he moaned, "I love you and miss you babe."

Sam cried, "Me too."

"Sam, don't worry I will be home soon."

"Thank You for using Securus, GOOD BYE…"

SILENT TREATMENT

Sergeant Gibson has been on the job for less than two years. The job had been rough for her, but she had been holding it down.

Damn, these niggas look good as hell, she constantly thought. Gibson gets turned on by the inmates in the facility where she works. So much that she finds herself going home and masturbating with them on her mind. There were a few potential men that she would love to give the pussy to. But she wouldn't take that risk. Well at least she thought.

One-night C.O Smith came into her office. "We have a new Inmate Serg," he said.

"Okay, bring him in, let me get his information."

"Mr. Scott right this way" Smith ordered.

The inmate came in and took a seat. Gibson's back was facing him.

"I don't know why I just can't go to my cell"
Shawn said.

"Relax sir, you will be in there soon." Sergeant
Gibson replied, "Okay, let's look at your paper
work"

"STACEY?" Shawn screamed out once Gibson
turned to face him.

Stacey looked up and was in shock.

"Shawn?" she asked in confusion.

The last time she had saw him was two
years ago. They were dating for nine months.
Then out of the blue she had not heard from
him.

"Stacey, girl I have been looking for you for
years. I miss you so much Baby." Shawn said
with excitement.

Stacey was happy to see him but then instantly
she had become upset.

"FUCK YOU SHAWN! I haven't seen or heard from you in two years. You woke up one morning and said that you would be back and never returned. So, fuck you Shawn" Stacey cried.

"Let me explain Stacey" he pleaded.

"NO, and please act like you don't know me. I will lose my job." Stacey yelled.

"C.O!" she called out, "take him to his cell."

***

Stacey went home with mixed feelings. Although she was angry, she had missed him. Her love life hadn't been the same since he left, and she hadn't slept with any one in two years. More than anything, she needed to know why he had left.

After morning count, she had Shawn brought to her office. She told the officer that she would bring him back to his cell. After they were given their privacy, Stacey turned to Shawn.

"Okay Explain"

Shawn explained the story leaving Stacey was upset and sad. All this time she had thought that he had played her.

"Do you forgive?" he asked once he finished his story.

Stacey looked at him with lust in her eyes. *Damn, he got my pussy so wet.* She thought to herself. She walked over to him with a straight face.

"Stand up!" she ordered.

"Stacey do you-" Shawn was interrupted.

"SERGEANT GIBSON" she yelled, correcting him.

Shawn looked at her in a strange way. She put the hand cuffs back on him. Every time he tried to speak, she had shut him down. She turned him around and took her night stick out. Shawn became nervous. Stacey stood behind him and rubbed the night stick up and down the side of his leg. With the other hand she unbuttoned her blouse, exposing her double D breast. Shawn's dick started to grow.

"Baby, pleaseee let me turn around" he begged.

"NO, be quiet." she demanded.

She put the night stick down and then pressed her body against his. She wrapped her arms around his waist and began to unbuckle his pants. Her hands found its way into his pants. *Damn, I forgot how big his dick was.* Her mouth began to water at her thoughts.

Shawn let out a soft moan while Stacey stroked his dick slowly.

"Stacey, please take these cuffs off, so I can show you how much I have missed you," he begged.

She didn't respond she just continued stroking. She then turned him around. He was so turned on by her. Looking at her breast and how hard her nipples were caused his dick to begin to jump.

Seeing this put a smile on her face. *GOT EM,* she thought.

Stacey put a chair in front of him. She lifted her skirt and pulled her thong to the side. Her pussy was soak and wet. She placed one leg over the arm rest exposing her wet dripping pussy. Shawn became super excited.

"Baby, I'm begging you take these off. Let me make you cum like how I used to."

Stacey started having flash backs of the nights when they used to fuck all over the house.

Stacey was thinking about taking off the cuffs, but she decided not to.

"Fuck it let him suffer" she whispered to herself.

She slid the seat closer to him. She then grabbed his dick roughly and started licking on the head of his dick. She went from side to side and then she put the whole thing in her mouth.

"I miss the way you suck this dick. Don't stop Stace." He moaned.

Stacey missed it as well. She was going fast. Her mouth was so watery. When she looked up spit was dripping from her chin. She then leaned back in the chair. She took two fingers and started sucking on them. She pinched on her nipples as she moaned. She spread her pussy lips to show off her pink clit. She massaged it slowly. Then she pushed the same two fingers inside of her. Slowly she pushed in and out. The whole time she was looking into Shawn's eyes. This was making him hornier. Shawn dropped to his knees and put in face between Stacey's legs. Shawn started licking on her clit and sucking all her juices.

"Shawn, I missed you daddy" she whispered.

Stacey began to grind her pussy in his face when she felt all her juices about to come down.

KNOCK, KNOCK, KNOCK

"Sergeant, count is about to begin," an officer informed her.

"I'm coming" she answered quickly.

"Don't stop Shawn" she commanded in between moans. She started grinding faster. Her cries were so loud that she had to cover her mouth. Suddenly, she whispered, "I'm cummin Shawn. I'm cummin."

She exploded in his mouth. Her body was weak. Shawn looked up at her.

"Okay baby take these cuffs off of me so I can fuck the shit out of you," he suggested.

"Shawn, you didn't hear? It's count time," Stacey said fixing her clothes.

"Let's go inmate" She demanded.

She fixed his clothes.

"You can't leave me like this Stace, you got my dick hurting."

"Sorry Shawn, I can't help you right now," Stacey replied.

"OFFICER!" She yelled, "take him to his cell for count" she said. Shawn looked at her in disbelief.

As Shawn was walking out the door, Stacey spoke.

"Mr. Scott, tomorrow we will talk about what activities you can do for good behavior," she said.

Shawn smiled, "Yes Sergeant Gibson......"

SISTERLY LOVE

Kisha and Trisha found themselves in a jam. Kisha was doing a favor for her boyfriend by dropping off a bag. She asked Trisha to come for the ride since the drop was only two hours away. Kisha and Trisha had been best friends since junior high school. They knew everything about each other, so of course Trisha agreed to roll when her best friend when she had asked her.

"I don't know why we had to drive out here so late Kish. This shit couldn't wait until the morning?" Trisha asked.

"Noo girl. Look, don't start with your complaining and questioning just relax and enjoy the ride" Kisha said.

They stopped at the gas station, filled up the tank, got some drinks for the road and some Backwoods to smoke. They were on the way to Albany. They laughed, sang, drunk and smoked all the way there.

"Damn Kish, slow down you just almost hit that car." Trisha told her.

"I'm good girl just relax."

Kisha's vision was a little blurry. She swerved again, this time she almost hit a cop cruiser.

"KISHA!" Trisha screamed out, "you almost hit that cop car. Pull over I'm driving." Trisha ordered. Just then the police car pulled up behind them with their lights flashing.

"Oh my God, this can't be happening," Kisha said in a nervous tone, "Anthony's going to kill me."

"License Registration Ma'am" The officer requested.

"Here you go officer, I was trying not to hit the possum in the middle of the road." Kisha explain immediately.

"Ma'am there was no possum on the road. Were you ladies drinking?" He asked as he looked at the bottle of Hennessy on the car floor.

"No Sir," Trisha yelled.

"Step out of the car ladies," the officer on the other side of the car demanded.

Kisha was terrified because she knew what was in the bag but never told her B.F.F.

"Well look what we have here," one officer said. He took the duffle bag out of the car and placed it onto the hood. When he opened it, he saw ten pounds of marijuana. Trisha eyes opened wide. She looked at Kisha.

"WHAT THE FUCK IS THIS KISHA?" She screamed.

Kisha couldn't say a word.

"Be quiet, you both are going to the county jail," one officer said while him and his partner put the two girls in cuffs.

Kisha still hadn't said a word and Trisha was crying out of control.

The officers took them to the county jail where they stayed for a few months until they got sentence to three years. Trisha hadn't spoken to Kisha since the night of their arrest. She was so mad at her B.F.F. She didn't understand why she hadn't told her what was in the bag so that she would have known how to travel. For Kisha, seeing Trisha every day and not speaking was killing her. She needed her friend. Those bitches in the prison were crazy. Kisha had one girl eat her out and now the girl was in love.

I need my sister to talk to me, she thought. She requested to switch beds with another inmate by paying her with cigarettes just to be in the same cell with Trisha.

Trisha was in the yard when the switch was made. By the time she had finished talking to the other inmates it was lights out. She went back to her cell and her "bunky" was already sleep. Trisha laid in the bed, but she couldn't sleep. She thought about her boyfriend a lot. She even masturbated from time to time. This was one of those nights where she needed to. She had pulled both of her breast out and started to rub them. She pinched on her nipples lightly. She gave a soft moan. She didn't want her cellmate to hear her, but Kisha had already heard the moans. It started turning her on. Trisha then pulled her panties down half way. She spread her legs just enough to feel the juices spilling out from her pussy. She split her lips apart and began to rub her clit very gently in slow motions. Her pussy was soak and wet, she was heaven.

She continued to rub. The whole time her eyes were closed. Seeing the image of her boyfriend's face made her pussy jump. She was so into it that she didn't even hear Kisha come down from the top bunk. Kisha was fully naked. She watched Trisha for a little while before she touched her leg. Trisha jumped up feeling embarrassed. When she saw Kisha she was relieved and upset at the same time.

"What are you doing here Kisha?" she whispered. Trisha grabbed her sheet and wrapped it around her.

"Trish, please accept my apology, I'm sorry. I know I should have told you. Please forgive me." Kisha pleaded. Kisha pulled the sheet off the top bunk and wrapped it around her body as well.

Trisha did miss her best friend.

"I forgive you Kish" she said with a smile on her face.

Kisha was so happy that she gave Trisha a hug.

"I miss you B.F.F." Kisha whispered in her ear. Trisha was still hot and horny. Her pussy was soak and wet. Her and Kisha had experimented from time to time with each other, so Trisha thought that Kisha had some making up to do.

"You do? Show me how much Kish," Trisha said while rubbing on Kisha's ass.

Kisha began kissing on her neck and gently rubbing on her breast. She kissed all over Trisha until she got to her breast.

She began to flick her tongue back and forth on her nipples. Trisha was so excited.

"Damn, this feel good" she moaned.

Kisha spread Trisha's legs opened. When she touched Trisha's pussy, she was amazed at how wet it was. She stuck one finger in at first, then two. She moved them in and out. Kisha licked up and down Trisha's stomach until she got to her destination. She took both hands and opened Trish's lips and then started licking and sucking on her clit. Trisha moaned and grabbed Kisha by the back of her head, grinding her pussy into her mouth.

Kisha stuck her tongue deep inside of Trisha. She sucked all her juices out. Kisha licked all the way back to her neck then gave her a long kiss. Kisha opened her legs and climbed on top of her, positioning herself until both of their clits were touching each other. They began to grind their clits together and pinch each other's nipples. Their moans were becoming louder. "Trisha, I'm about to cum." Kisha said "Me too." Trish replied.

They grinded faster and faster until the they both exploded. Kisha laid next to Trisha. She was all out of breath. They both needed to release some tension. Kisha looked at Trisha. "B.F.F for life?" she asked.

"B.F.F for life," Trisha replied…

OBEY MY RULES

C.O Watson was one of the meanest in the house. He fussed about everything in the Rosemary Singer House at Rikers Island Facility. He had worked in that building for four years. Some of the ladies could not stand him, while others were in love with him. C.O Watson was six feet tall. He had brown skin with a great build. Some have said that he favors Tyson Beckford, the model. He knew that he looked good so, he used that to his advantage.

Watson had slept with several inmates over the course of the years. He would tell them things that they had wanted and needed to hear. One time he had told an inmate that if she had slept with him then her time would have been reduced. She was sent upstate shortly after. He had been fucking two inmates, Michelle and Natasha. Every Monday, Wednesday, and Friday he snuck into Michelle's cell, bent her over and fucked the shit out of her. On Tuesdays, Thursdays, and Saturdays he would wake Tasha up by putting his dick into her mouth. She would suck it until he busted. On Sundays, he rested.

One Sunday, Watson was stuck doing a double shift since staff was short. It was a long day. Watson was finally relaxing in the office. He put on a movie. His mind was racing, he was deep in thought. *Which one of these broads will I take out of their cell? Michelle got some good ass pussy but, Natasha's head game is out of control.* The thought of them both had his dick rock hard.

"I know what to do," he mumbled to himself. Watson went and got Michelle and Natasha from their cells. The ladies looked at each other. They both were confused as to why they were called to the office.

"Ok Watson, why am I here?" Michelle asked Watson as he looked at her in a strange way.

"Yes Watson, why am I here as well?" Natasha asked after Michelle.

Watson looked at them both for a minute and then chuckled.

"Tonight. I want to do things differently. I want to enjoy both of you ladies at the same time," Watson replied.

Natasha looked at Watson and then at Michelle. "Sorry I don't get down like that." She said nervously.

Michelle was down with anything. When she worked at the strip club, before she was sentenced, she always performed with other females. It used to get very nasty. Watson was disappointed with Natasha's answer.

"All I have done for you. Making sure you were good, the extra phone calls, the giving you this good." Watson said.

Natasha looked at him with lust in her eyes. Yes, he had done a lot for and she didn't want it to stop. "Okay, I'll do it." She said.

Watson smiled with enjoyment. He motioned for Michelle to go kiss Natasha. Michelle walked over without saying a word. She stroked Natasha's long hair.

"You have some beautiful hair" Michelle said.

"Thank you" Natasha replied.

Michelle tilted her head back and then started kissing on her neck. Natasha's eyes rolled to the back of her head. Every kiss Michelle gave felt so good, her panties was getting moist.

Michelle licked up and down Natasha's neck. She even started sucking on her earlobe. She then licked her lips. Gently she stuck her tongue into her mouth. They began to kiss slowly. Michelle started to unbutton Natasha's jumper.

This exposed her breast. She rubbed on her nipples. Natasha started to moan. Watson stood there and watched while his dick began to grow. Michelle laid Natasha onto the desk and then started sucking and biting on her nipples. She spread her legs apart and pushed Natasha's panties to the side.

"Damn, you're so wet." Michelle said.

"Watson you want to feel how wet she is?" She asked.

Watson was stroking his dick.

"Yes, yes" He replied with excitement.

When he walked over Michelle pushed him down onto his knees.

"Damn that's a pretty pussy" he said.

"Taste it" Natasha whispered while rubbing on her own breast.

Watson spread Natasha's legs wider and then pushed his whole face in her pussy. He opened her lips and sucked all the juices out of her. That drove Natasha crazy. Michelle took her jumper off and started playing with herself. Watching Michelle play with herself was turning Natasha on further.

She had never been with a female before but looking at Michelle was very tempting. Natasha grabbed Michelle by the hand and pulled her close to her face. Michelle put one leg up on the desk.

Natasha began to lick on her pussy. Gently she licked and sucked on her clit. Michelle started grinding her hips. Natasha grabbed Michelle's waist and placed her on top of her face so that she could truly enjoy sucking all of Michelle's juices out. Watson stepped back to watch Michelle and Natasha enjoy each other. *My dream is finally coming true,* Watson thought to his self. He inserted his dick inside of Natasha while she was still sucking on Michelle's clit. She let out a loud moan. Watson started off his motions slow, going in and out. His eyes rolled to the back off his head. He was in heaven. He pulled Michelle's hair from the back and then started tonguing her down.

Michelle felt her body starting to tingle. She started moaning out of control. She rode Natasha's face faster. She was sucking her pussy so good, she couldn't control her feelings.

Watson began to fuck Natasha harder. The smell of sex filled the air. It looked like a scene straight from a porno.

"Bitch, you about to make me cum" Michelle said while still riding Natasha's face.

"Cum girl, I want to hear you" Watson whispered as he was about to cum himself.

Michelle was grinding faster and faster. Chills took over her body and her nipples became so hard.

"I'M CUMMIN!" She yelled.

"FUCK ME TOO!" Watson said out loud.

Just like that, the party of three released their juices and then collapsed onto each other.

"This was great ladies. Same time next Sunday?" Watson asked.

Michelle and Natasha just looked at each other and laughed…

D.O.C WIFE'S CLUB

Every other Saturday a group of ladies, Amanda, Cynthia, Yvette, Monique, Karlie, and the new-comer Shonette, would meet up to catch a bus that goes to Sing Sing Correctional Facility to see their husbands. The ladies had been going up to the prison together for the past three years. Except Shonette, she had only been going for one year. These ladies formed a bond. All of them was going through the same thing.

"Heyy ladies" Monique yelled.

"Hey Mo" the ladies said in return.

"How was everyone's week?" she asked.

"Crazy" Cynthia said, "kids driving me crazy, job stressing me out, plus I had to run around for my husband's package. I really need a day of relaxation."

All the ladies were shaking their heads.

"Well, I guess we all had the same exact week." Shonette replied.

"Yes, I totally agree, a day of relaxation is long over do." Amanda said.

"I may have something in mind but let's discuss it after our visits." Monique suggested

All the ladies were so excited to see their husbands and their boyfriends. They all had an ear full to tell.

***

"So, babe, I was thinking about inviting the ladies to one of my events. They're complaining about needing a day of fun and relaxation. What you think?" Monique asked. Monique's husband looked at her like she was crazy. He was the type that didn't want her to converse with no one up there.

"Babe, I keep telling you. Stop making new friends. Can you trust these ladies? This is not just a regular party. You sure you ready for people to be in your business?" He asked.

"These ladies have been my support team since I met them up here. We are all going through it. We are lonely and missing our men. And you know anybody that comes to these events must sign a disclosure." She explained.

"Okay babe, you know best," he replied.

"TIMES UP!" The C.O yelled.

"Damn this time go so fast. I love you baby." Monique said.

"Love you too" her husband replied, "I'll call you tonight."

The ladies got back on the bus. They had a lot to talk about.

"Okay ladies, I have an event every month. It's a private event for ladies only. You can say it's like a toy party or a pleasure party some people may call it. Now, you must sign a disclosure before coming. What happens there, stays there. You have a few days to think about." Monique explained.

"A disclosure? All of that just for a party? Who do you think you are? Beyonce?" Amanda questioned.

"Look, you don't have to come. Everyone else if you're interested let me know."

They rode back to Brooklyn in silence.

***

Two days before the event, Monique had heard from the ladies. They all agreed to attend. She was excited. She had an extra special treat for them. The night was finally here. Monique had a bar full of different drinks. The bar tenders wore nothing but body paint. She had a table full of desserts and appetizers. Her last table was full of different pleasure toys for the ladies. She hired somebody to give full body massages and she had two female strippers. Finally, her guest had arrived.

"Hey ladies, welcome, welcome" Monique said.

"Girl, this house is dope. I thought the event was in your house." Shonette said.

"NO, for these events I rent out spaces. It's better because it has a lot of room." Monique explained, "anyway, come on in. We have bartenders, food and other treats you can enjoy. Introduce yourself to the other ladies. Relax we're going to enjoy the night."

The ladies looked around in amazement. Some of them was already turned on.

May I have everyone's attention?" Mo asked. "I'd like to thank all of my ladies for coming. Some of you are regulars but we have a few new ones today. We must make them feel at home. Now ladies, like I explained before, this is a private event. What happens here stays here. Now that I got that out the way. Let me introduce you to our massage therapist for the evening. This is Rachel, she does wonders." Rachel was a 5'10, brown skin female with long hair. Her shape was bananas. She had a small waist with some thick ass thighs.

Monique continued, "our sexy bartenders are Cinnamon and Spice. They make the best drinks in the world. I have a special treat, but we will save that for later. Let's mingle ladies."

The ladies were impressed. Amanda and Shonette walked over to a table that had different lotions and creams on top of it.

"I want to know what this do" Amanda said while picking up one of the jars of cream.

"Oh, that cream you put some on your clit and it stimulates it," one of the guests explained, "you should try it, it works wonders."

Amanda and Shonette took her advice and went into the bathroom to apply the cream.

"This shit is not going to work, we're wasting our time" Shonette said.

***

All the ladies were getting drunk and having a good time.

"I'm ready for a massage. I am long over do for one." Amanda said, "Rachel, I'm ready for your special massage."

"Great! Do you want to do it in front of everybody or in a private setting?" Rachel asked

"Out here is fine I don't have anything to hide."

Rachel told Amanda to go upstairs to take a quick shower to rinse all the lotion she had on off her skin. Amanda did what was told and then went back downstairs.

"Okay ladies, we have our first participant for our massage." Rachel announced.

"Wait, let me get another drink. This drink is so good. I don't know what you mixed in here but it's hitting the spot." Amanda said to Cinnamon who just winked her eye at her.

Rachel instructed Amanda to lay on the table on her back and to remove the towel. Amanda did what she was told. Rachel opened her suit case. She had different types of essential oils.

"This fist oil I will apply is peppermint oil, this helps with tension." She explained.

Rachel started with Amanda shoulders. She then moved to her arms and then her stomach. She cupped her breast, massaged around them and then she began to pinch her nipples. Amanda let out a moan. Rachel did that for a few minutes then proceeded to massage the rest of her body. Amanda was in heaven. Her body was relaxed, and the drinks were kicking in. She was becoming horny.

"Who would like to help me, it's great when you're getting a massage from several hands. Whomever else wants a massage as well please go rinse the lotion off your skin. While the other ladies massage Amanda, I can start on you," Rachel said.

Shonette, Cynthia, Yvette, and Karlie all ran upstairs to rinse their skin. All the ladies were ready for their massages. Looking at Amanda get hers did something to them. As they were coming down stairs, they couldn't believe what they were seeing. Monique and two other females were all over Amanda. One was sucking on her breast. One was kissing her, and Monique was eating her out. Shonette was opened from what she was watching. The other girls were still amazed.

"Come down ladies join us. Who is next for a massage?" Rachel asked.

Shonette jumped on the table and prepared herself for the treatment. Rachel started rubbing all over her. She motioned for Yvette, Karlie and Cynthia to help.

Cynthia was rubbing her thighs. Karlie was pinching and sucking on her breast and Karlie was rubbing on the rest of her body. Cynthia spread Shonette's legs apart to see a pretty pink wet pussy. She stuck two fingers inside of it and began to finger fuck her.

"Mmmm, yes!" Shonettte whispered.

Karlie started licking on her clit while Cynthia was fingering her. On the other table Monique was now laying on it and Amanda was on top of her. They were grinding their pussies together. Monique had one guest sit on her face and she stuck her tongue deep inside her pussy. She slurped as she sucked all the juices out.

Rachel had one girl on the steps with her legs in the air. She was fucking her with a strap on. Yvette went to the table with all the toys and grabbed a vibrator. She sat on the couch and spread her legs and began to play with herself. Cinnamon and Spice joined the action. Spice laid Cinnamon onto the bar. She put whip cream all over her and started to lick it off her. Everybody was having such a great time that Monique had forgotten about the strippers. When she turned to look for them, they had two of the ladies bent over fucking them with dildos.

All the ladies were all over the house. These ladies had never experienced anything like this, but they were enjoying it. Cynthia and Karlie were fucking each other with a two headed dildo and kissing each at the same time. Monique walked over to Shonette and grabbed her.

"Come here, I wanted you for the longest." Monique said.

Monique dropped to her knees and started eating the shit out of her friend. Shonette took her head and pushed it further between her legs. She was grinding her pussy so fast on her until she exploded all over. Monique put the strap on and told her, "come suck on this dick." Shonette was sucking that strap on like it was her boyfriend's dick. While she was sucking, she put two fingers in Monique and one in her ass. She was finger fucking her hard and fast.

Monique was moving and screaming out of control. Her sounds made everybody more excited. One by one the ladies screamed out. "I'M CUMMIN!"

They were out of breath and couldn't believe what had just taken place. Now they understood why Monique wanted them to sign a disclosure. This was something that they could get used to.

"So, when is our next meeting?" Karlie blurted out.

They all laughed…

THE MORE, THE MERRIER

A couple of officers went to a bar downtown for one of their colleagues. She had just received a big promotion at work. For events like this the department booked a few rooms at the Marriott on Adam Street.

"Congratulations to Officer Charlene for a job well done and for becoming Captain."

One of the officers yelled out. Everyone screamed and shouted, congratulating her. Some of the other female officers was hating on her. Rumor had it that she was fucking all the top bosses. That's how she got all her over time, vacations and now this promotion.

Some of the rumors were true but she didn't care. Before she became an officer, she was a stripper down in North Carolina and from time to time she had done private shows. Only one other officer knew that, Tim. Charlene and Tim fucked a few times. Sometimes it got very kinky.

"Hey, miss lady how you feel about getting this promotion?" Tim asked.

"It feels good, I mean, I worked my ass off for this position" Charlene replied.

"Well, we need to really celebrate after if you're not busy" he said.

Charlene laughed, "we're celebrating now" she replied.

"You know what I mean Char."

"Let's see how the night goes," she stated

***

Everyone was having a good time. It was an open bar event with free food. People was hooking up with each other and leaving. Charlene was completely wasted, she danced with Tim and Marcus all night. Marcus was her co-worker who worked on her shift. They never did anything but just send each other nude pictures and videos. Tim and Marcus had Charlene in a sandwich, they were grinding on her. Charlene started to become horny. She grabbed on Tim's dick secretly.

"It's time to continue this party elsewhere," Charlene said.

Tim gave a little smile. Charlene turned to Marcus, grabbed on his dick and then asked.

"You coming?"

Marcus looked shocked. He looked at Tim and Tim nodded to give him the okay to join.

"Let's go" Marcus replied.

Charlene instructed the men to meet her in the lobby of the Marriott. She was going to say bye to everyone and collect her gifts.

"Thanks everyone for celebrating with me. But it is time for me to go. I'm way too drunk."

"Hey, Char you need help to the hotel? I have a room in there too." Crystal asked.

"Sure, love" Charlene said.

As she looked at Crystal, she started thinking.

Damn she looks good and I bet you she tastes sweet.

The ladies walked to the hotel. Marcus and Tim were waiting in the lobby.

"What's up Crystal what are you doing here?" Marcus asked.

"I have a room here. I was not going to be drunk on nobody train. What are you doing here?" She asked Marcus.

Marcus was about to answer but before he did Charlene spoke.

"They going to the after party, you wanna come?"

Marcus was shocked, Tim was excited, and Crystal smiled.

"Sure, whose going?" She asked.

"Just us four, it's in my room." Char responded.

The four of them rode the elevator to the 23rd floor.

"Here we are room 2301. Now before we enter, I must say what happens here stays here agreed?" Charlene asked. Everyone nodded their heads yes. They entered the room and got comfy. Charlene had drinks in the room and snacks. They drunk some more, played music and danced.

"It's so hot in here," Charlene said as she took off her dress and danced around in her bra and panties. She grabbed Marcus and started dancing to R. Kelly's song, "Seems like you're ready." They began to grind on each other. Marcus turned her around and then bent her over. He held onto her waist and then continued to grind on her ass. She stood up as he grabbed her breast. Tim walked over and stood in front of her. He grinded on her as well. He pulled her breast out of her bra and then began to lick on her nipples.

He slid his hands down her panties and started fingering her. Charlene was in heaven. Marcus was kissing on her neck. Crystal couldn't believe what she was watching. But she was getting turned on by it. Tim dropped to his knees, pulled her panties down, opened her legs and then put his tongue inside of her pussy. Charlene grabbed the back of his head and pushed it in more. Marcus was rubbing on her breast and pinching her nipples. Charlene stretched her hand out to Crystal. Crystal stood up from the bed and walked over to her. Charlene started kissing on her neck. Tim took her bra off. Crystal was in shock from what was going on.

She wanted them to stop but it was feeling too good. She never did anything crazy like this, so she was going to blame it on the liquor. Charlene and Crystal began to kiss. Charlene pushed her onto the bed and then climbed on top of her and continued to kiss her. Marcus and Tim were amazed by what they were watching. Charlene took one hand and put it down her panties and began to rub on her clit. Crystal let out a moan.

"Mmmmm, her pussy's so wet." Charlene whispered.

"Marcus come feel this." She said.

Marcus walked with excitement. He spread Crystal's legs open. He then kissed between her thighs until he got where he needed to be. He gave her pussy one lick.

"You're right, it is wet." He said.

He continued to lick and suck on her pussy and clit. Charlene moved up to Crystal's face. Crystal was nervous, she didn't know what to do so she closed her eyes. Super turned on by what Marcus was doing to her, she grabbed Charlene by her ass and pushed her pussy in her face, and just like that Crystal went to work. She stuck her tongue inside of Charlene, going in and out until Charlene began to grind on her tongue. Crystal never knew pussy could taste so sweet. Tim walked over to Charlene and started sucking on her breast while he jerked his dick.

Charlene grabbed Tim's dick, placed it in her mouth and slowly started sucking on it. Tim closed his eyes and leaned his head back. He was in heaven. The moans and groans in the room was turning them on. Marcus stuck his penis inside of Crystal so deep that she started screaming. He was fucking her so hard. Charlene turned around while still sitting on Crystal's face. She wanted to watch while Marcus was fucking her. Charlene opened Crystal's legs wider so that she could lick her while Marcus was inside of her. Tim climbed behind Charlene and entered her slow.

"Damn, this pussy tight" he mumbled.

All of them was in tune with each other. Their moans grew louder and louder. One by one they exploded, releasing every ounce of juice they had in their bodies.

Crystal was speechless, she had never done anything like this. Not even with her own boyfriend. Although it was new, she loved every bit of it. She was still turned on. The high from what she had just experienced left her out of breath. After catching her breath, she finally spoke.

"Let's do it again…"

THE NIGHT OF NEW BEGINNINGS

It was January 25th. Midnight to be exact and Cassie was waiting at the gates of Down State Correctional Facility. Today was the day her Melvin was finally being release after three years in prison. It was a Friday night, so he wasn't due to see his parole officer until Monday morning. She didn't tell the rest of the family that he was coming home because she wanted time for just them two. She already knew that wasn't happening once he got home. Cassie hired a driver to drive a sprinter to pick up and drop them to their destination. She had his favorite drink and some food waiting for him. A half an hour had passed, and she was getting nervous.

"Let me call this jail" she said to herself.

Just then, the gates had opened.

There he was. 5'10, brown skin, built and solid. Cassie smiled and cried out of control. Her Poppi was out. Melvin was excited to see his girl as well. She jumped out of the sprinter and ran to him. She hugged and kissed him all over.

"HI POPPI!" Cassie said.

"Hey Babe" Melvin replied.

They got into the sprinter and began their journey.

"Hey Mike, please take us back to the hotel." Cassie instructed.

"Hotel?" Mike questioned.

"Yes, I have a room for the night before we go home. I have a few surprises for you Poppi" Cassie explained.

All Melvin could do was smile. Cassie was all over him on their ride there. She looked in his eyes and said, "I missed you so much." Melvin looked at his girl, he missed her as well.

"Show me" he told her.

Cassie climbed on top of Melvin's lap and then began to kiss on his neck. Their lip's locked. The kiss was so passionate. Cassie never kissed Melvin like that. It was something she had been longing to do. Melvin slid his hand underneath her dress. He was in amazement.

"No panties huh?" he asked.

Cassie smiled as she unbuckled his pants. Melvin took one of her breast's out and began to lick and bite on her nipples.

Cassie was in heaven. Before he could slide in her, Cassie's juices were coming down her leg. This turned Melvin on. He was ready to fuck the shit out of her.

"We are here" Mike, the driver, said.

Cassie and Melvin fixed themselves up and then exited the sprinter.

"Thanks Mike, see you in the morning" Cassie said before entering the hotel.

Cassie had already set up everything before picking Melvin up.

"Babe, why didn't we go straight home?" Melvin questioned.

"No questions." Cassie said, "tonight Poppi it's about you. Turn around I need to put this blindfold on you" she instructed.

"What? For what?"

Melvin wasn't with this game. Cassie laughed.

"Just turn around please. Or are you too thug to play this game," she asked jokingly.

Melvin looked at her in a nervous way but played along. She put the blindfold on him, grabbed his hand and then lead him towards the room.

"Cee, I don't like this" Melvin said.

"Relax babe, I just need you to trust me" she replied.

She opened the room door. The smell of a sweet scent hit Melvin's nose. Trey Songz was playing.

"Okay Poppi, before I take off your blindfold let me just say that since we can't go away to D.R I decided to bring D.R to us. Tonight, is about you and I want you to have the time of your life." Cassie explained, "take a sip."

Cassie put a glass of Patron to his mouth so that he could drink some. Melvin's heart was racing because he didn't know what to expect. Just then, two Dominican chicks came out of the bathroom with only thongs on. Cassie was already in her robe. She sat in the corner and watched them go to work on Melvin. She was nervous as well, but this was his fantasy and she wanted to experience with him. Melvin felt two sets of hands rubbing all over him. His dick instantly became hard. One lady took his pants off while the other took off his shirt.

One of them climbed on top of him and started to grind on him. The other female pushed his head back and put one of her breasts into his mouth. Melvin was in heaven. The music in the room grew louder. Cassie walked over and gave Melvin another sip of liquor. As Cassie walked away, she slapped one of the ladies' ass. The sound turned Melvin on even more.

"Come baby, take the blindfold off already," he begged.

"Not yet Poppi" she replied.

Cassie met the two girls, Maria and Jazmin, in Angels Strip Club one night and told them her plan. They were down with it from the jump only if she was joining in as well. She was going to join them, she just wanted Melvin to enjoy this moment. His fantasy was to have three females and he kept talking about going to D.R. Maria and Jazmin was sexy as hell. Cassie had never been with another female, but these two were turning her on. They laid Melvin on the bed. Cassie walked over took her robe off and joined them. Cassie took the blindfold off Melvin. He was in shock by what was going on. Maria and Jazmin were kissing each other on one side of the bed.

"Welcome home Poppi" Cassie whispered in his ear.

Melvin was still floored. He couldn't believe that Cassie had done this. For all the years they had been together they never discussed a threesome or anything of that nature. He knew right then that he had loved her more. Cassie started licking on his nipples and jerking his dick at the same time. She licked his chest, down his stomach until finally she stopped where she needed to be. She licked the head of his dick real slow and then gave it a kiss. "Damn, I missed you," she whispered.
She then slowly put all of Melvin into her mouth. At first, she was sucking it real slow then she started to move faster. Melvin was on cloud nine. He laid there with his eyes closed.

Maria walked over to Cassie, spread her pussy open and then started licking on her clit. Cassie began to moan. Melvin opened his eyes to see what was going on. He couldn't believe that his fantasy was coming true. Jazmin started licking on his dick with Cassie.

"What the fuck" Melvin yelled out.

He grabbed Cassie's head.

"Suck it baby" he demanded.

Cassie loved to be talked to dirty. She instructed Jazmin to ride Melvin's dick. Jazmin climbed on top while Jazmin was fucking him, Cassie and Maria were sucking and licking Jazmin's breast. Cassie laid Maria down next to Melvin. She started to tongue Maria down. The two ladies were grinding their pussies together. Cassie was so wet. She never thought that she would be doing any of this.

Her moans were becoming louder. Melvin was fucking Jazmin from behind. Then they switched. Jazmin started sucking on Cassie's clit and rubbing on her titties. Melvin was watching and loving every bit of it. Jazmin climbed to Cassie's face and then grinded her pussy in her mouth. Cassie sucked and tongue fucked Jazmin until she came.

Melvin grabbed Cassie by her neck and stuck his tongue down her throat.

"I fucking love you babe" he said.

"Shut and put that dick in my mouth," Cassie replied.

Melvin did just that. Jazmin spread Cassie's legs wide. Both ladies started kissing and licking her inner thighs. Maria stuck two fingers inside of her. Cassie moaned.

"Damn, this pussy tight" Maria said.

Jazmin sucked all of Cassie's juices out. Maria put on a strap on and fucked her. Cassie arched her back as soon as Maria entered her. This turned her on more. She was sucking Melvin's dick so wild. Melvin couldn't hold it anymore, so he busted in her mouth.

"FUCK" he screamed while holding the back of Cassie's head.

Without hesitation, Cassie swallowed all of him. Maria was still fucking her. Melvin's dick was still hard as hell and now he wanted to feel the inside of his girl. He kissed all over Cassie's body. He spread her legs and was sucking the shit out her pussy. Cassie was so amazed and excited. Never had they had sex this intense.

"Fuck me Poppi, please" she begged.

"You sure you're ready for that babe?" Melvin asked.

"Yesss Daddy" she replied

Melvin entered her real slow.

"Damn, I missed how wet this pussy gets," he mumbled.

He started off with slow long strokes. He was just enjoying the moment. He turned his head and saw Maria on her knees with her face between Jazmin legs. The moans from the two ladies and Cassie was making him hornier.

"Take everything that belongs to you Poppi" Cassie whispered.

Melvin turned Cassie around and then hit it from the back. He grabbed her vibrator, turned it on and then put it near her asshole. Cassie was loving all of this. She screamed out.

"Fuck me please."

Melvin started fucking her hard and fast. Just then Jazmin yelled out.

"FUCK I'M CUMMIN!"

The other two ladies were grinding on each other. Melvin watched them while he fucked the shit out of Cassie.

"Don't stop" Cassie yelled.

Melvin started to go faster. Cassie couldn't hold it any more.

"Baby I'm about to cum. Cum with me Poppi," she begged.

Cassie's walls tighten up around his dick. His body started to tingle. The faster he humped the more the sensation was growing.

"SHIT!!" Melvin shouted.

"Cum Baby, POPPI, I'm cummin"

Just then Cassie's juices squirted all over the place. Maria and Jazmin let out a moan. They came as well. Melvin exploded inside of Cassie and then collapsed on top of her. Everyone was drained and out of breath. With the little energy she had, she kissed Melvin on the forehead. "Welcome home Poppi…"

ME TIME...

It was another long day for Monica. She pulled another twelve-hour shift at her marketing firm. Ever since her husband became incarcerated two years ago, she kept herself extremely busy. She has eight-year-old twin boys, Joshua and Noah. They drive her crazy every chance they get. She's happy that tonight the boys were with her mom. She spoke to her husband, Brandon, before she walked in the door. Every time she spoke to him, it made her depressed. She came in, put her keys on the table and then checked her voicemail. She had two missed call from her best friend Karlie. Karlie was very supportive to her situation because she had just gone through the same thing. The only difference is that her husband finally came home.

"Hey girl, I'm returning your call, how are things going?" Monica asked Karlie.

"What's up girl? I'm over here cooking for this man. Since he's been home, I've been cheffin' it up," Karlie responded.

"I can't wait for Brandon to come home so I can chef it up for him. I've just been so depressed, so I've been staying busy at work. I haven't been out in a minute" Monica explained.

"You should check out the D.O.C Wife's Club. It's a private club but I can call someone to get you in. You cannot tell anyone about it. It's a secret club," Karlie said.

"A secret club? Karlie, I don't want to be a part of a group of women talking about how depressed they are cause their men are locked up. No thank you."

"Monica, it's not like that. They helped me. Trust me, it's not what you think."

"No thank you Karlie," Monica said in an annoyed tone.

"Alright, well think about and when you ready to get out of this depression call me," Karlie said before she hung up.

Monica laughed to herself, "I love my girl Karlie but she's crazy."

***

Monica decided to open a bottle of Pinot. She poured her a glass and then turned on water for a nice hot bubble bath. She turned on her Pandora. Luther Vandross' song "A House is not a Home" came through the speaker. Monica stepped into the steamy hot water and sat down. The heat from the water, made her nipples hard. Monica laid back and relaxed in the tub as she sipped her wine. She sang along with Luther.

She kept sipping and singing until she caught a little buzz from the wine. Keith Sweat began to sing. Monica closed her eyes and started to reminisce about making love to her husband. The water was getting cold, so her nipples stayed hard. She grabbed onto both breast and then proceed to rub and pinch on her nipples.

She let out a small moan. She took another sip of the wine. She continued to feel on her breast. She spread her legs apart. She stuck two fingers inside of her pushing the lukewarm water inside. She moved her fingers in and out slowly.

"This feels soo good" she said out loud.

Her motion became faster and her moans louder. Monica turned the water back on full force and then she slid down toward the facet. Positioning herself right underneath it. She placed one leg over the tub railing so that her legs could be wide open. Monica proceeded to fondle her breast again squeezing each nipple.

The wine had gotten to her head. She was feeling tipsy and real horny. She ran her hand down her stomach until she reached between her legs. She spread open her pussy lips until her clit was in clear view. She slid down a little more until the hot water poured down right onto her pussy. The pressure of the water was getting her more aroused.

"Yes, yes make this pussy cum" she said to herself.

Her clit became swollen. Monica started to feel a little tingle between her legs, and she knew what that meant. She started to grind her hips to move back and forth making the water go up and down. She let out a scream when the tingling feeling was getting more intense. She grinded faster and faster while still pinching on her nipples.

"I'm cummin. I'm cummin."

Monica squirted all over the place. She got out of the tub and rushed to her night stand. She opened the draw and pulled out her sugar spoon vibrator and some lubricant. She grabbed the baby oil and rubbed it all over her body. Massaging each breast at a time nice and slow. She rubbed some on her ass and between her thighs. She laid on her back, turned the vibrator on and then placed it on her nipples to let the vibration turn her on. She moved it all over her body until she placed it where she needed it to be. Monica's pussy was already dripping wet.

The vibrating feeling was making her more wet, so she inserted her toy in side of her. She began to grind her hips, she was so turned on. Every time she closed her eyes, she saw images of her husband. Oh, how she craved for him. She slid the vibrator out and placed it on the tip of her clit, slowly moving it back and forth. Her body started to tingle again, and she knew what that meant. She began to speed up the motion of the vibrator. Her motions were becoming faster and faster, until she let out a scream. All her juices poured out of her body. She was trying to catch her breath. She needed to release all of that backed up tension. As she was laying in the bed, she started to think.

Maybe I will check out the D.O.C Wife's Club…

WATCHING YOU

Bedford Hills Correctional facility is a prison for women. Dominique was the overnight officer in house B. Usually there would be three officers but due to job cuts, she was the only one to patrol a house of twenty inmates. Nothing crazy ever went on in the house except for hearing a little noise from time to time. Shanise and Michelle were cellmates but also lovers. They both had a sentence of ten to twelve years. Every now and then they would fight and argue because Shanise would always flirt with another inmate. Shanise had a crush on Dominique but never said anything because she knew Michelle would have had a heart attack.

She would always give Dominique a compliment when she got her hair or nails done, or she would come up with random conversation just so she can be in her presence. One day she asked to speak to her in private. Dominique took Shanise in the office.

"How can I be of some assistance Shanise?" Dominique asked.

Shanise put her head down, "there are some things I need to get off my chest. I thank you for always being kind to us and treating us with respect." Shanise stated.

"Oh, that's no problem, I'm not gonna treat you like an animal just because you're in here." Dominique replied.

"Wait, I'm not finished," Shanise interrupted her.

She stood up and said "I've been fantasizing about you lately. I have just been wondering how your body feels, how you taste, if your lips are soft. Just by looking at you, my pussy always become moist." Shanise explained.

Dominique's mouth dropped. Not really knowing what to say she forced anything out. "Wow, I'm flattered but I'm married Shanise and I'm not gonna risk my job for anything." Just then Shanise walked over to her and kissed her. By surprise Dominique didn't resist, she kissed her back. Secretly Domonique had always thought that Shanise was so gorgeous. Dominique came to her senses and pushed Shanise off her.

"I'm sorry we cannot do this, I must take you back now," Dominique said.

Shanise smiled, she knew that Dominique wanted her too. She took her back to her cell and went back to her post.

***

All evening Domonique was thinking about what happen in the office. *Why didn't I stop her?* She thought. *Damn her lips were so soft.* She was very turned on by what happened. She tried not to think about.

"Okay ladies lights out" she yelled.

The night seemed to be dragging. Dominique started to doze off when she began to hear moans coming from one of the cells. She walked towards the noise. When she found the cell, she stopped in front of it and didn't say a word. She stood there and watched Shanise and Michelle get intimate. She stared at their naked bodies and how perfect both of their shapes were. She watched as Michelle placed Shanise's breast in her mouth and sucked on it slowly. She took her time to lick each nipple.

Shanise took Michelle by her face and began to tongue her down. She flipped her over and spread her legs wide. Shanise rubbed on Michelle's clit and felt the juice flow out of her. "Damn you're so wet" she whispered to Michelle.

She spread open her lips and slightly brushed her tongue across her clit teasing Michelle. Michelle let out a moan. She stuffed her face in Michelle's pussy and began to eat away. That drove Michelle crazy. She grabbed Shanise by her head and pushed her face in more. Dominique was so turned on she felt the moisture between her legs. Shanise got up and positioned herself on Michelle's face. Facing towards the gate, when she looked up, she saw Dominique standing there. She gave her a little smile.

Dominique's whole body froze. She couldn't move once Shanise saw her standing there. Shanise grinded her pussy on Michelle's mouth slowly and squeezed on her breast. Shanise took her left breast, put it in her mouth and bit on her nipple. She then did the same to the right one. Dominique was horny, just by watching them she wanted to cum so bad. She knew she was taking a risk, but she couldn't hold it. She leaned on the railing in front of Shanise's cell. She unbuckled her pants and slid her hands between her legs. Shanise never took her eyes off her.

Craving her more and more. Shanise opened Michelle's legs and rubbed on her clit, she patted it. She stuck two fingers inside her and took it out. Shanise licked all of Michelle's juices off her fingers. Dominique kept watching and rubbing on her pussy at the same time. She was soak and wet. Secretly Shanise and Dominque craved each other. Shanise started to grind faster on Michelle. Michelle was licking and sucking every juice out of Shanise.

The harder Shanise rubbed Michelle's clit the faster Dominique rubbed on hers. She knew that this was about to come to an end. Shanise and Dominique never took their eyes off each other. Dominique wanted to experience everything Michelle was feeling, and she wanted to taste Shanise so bad.

"I'm cummin baby" Shanise moaned.

Dominique felt it too and just like that the ladies had an orgasm. Dominique let out a slight moan but had to cover her mouth. She quickly fixed herself up and walked away. Michelle jumped up and looked towards the gate.

"Did you hear that?" She asked.

"Hear what?" Shanise responded.

"It sounded like someone else was here with us" Michelle said.

"Babe you're buggin, that was your moans echoing," she laughed.

Michelle never knew that Dominique was there that night and every other night after. Shanise knew that she couldn't really have her but just watching her play with herself was enough for now. She knew that she would get her one day. But just knowing that they had this little secret always made her smile and she loved it…

DADDY'S HOME

Terrance had been locked up for two years but he's finally going home to his wife and kids. He told his wife that he would be home in three days. He gave her the wrong date so that he could surprise her. The prison let him out at midnight, so he didn't get home until three in the morning. He still had his keys when they gave him back his property, so he was able to get in the house. The house was pitch black when he opened the door. The first room he went into was the kids. They were knocked out.

"My babies," he said.

He walked into his room. Terrance stared at his wife. He was just amazed at how beautiful she looked in her sleep. He wanted to jump all over her but first he had to take his jail clothes off, throw them in the trash and take a shower. Tiara jumped out of her sleep because she thought that she had heard the shower running.

"My mind is really playing tricks on me," she said lowly.

She laid back down and began to fall asleep. Just then her room door opened. Tiara didn't think to turn around because the kids would come in her room every night to lay with her.

"Go back in your bed, Mommy wants to lay by herself," she shouted.

Disregarding what she said, they still climbed in her bed.

"I said, go in your bed," she repeated.

Terrance finally spoke, "you sure you want me to sleep in the kids' room?"

The sounds of Terrance's voice startled her that she jumped out the bed and turned on the light.

Terrance sat up. Tiara's vision was blurry at first but when it became clear she couldn't believe what she was seeing.

"Terrance!" she cried out. She hopped back on the bed and began to hug him.

"Baby, what you are doing here? You said three more days."

"Surprise, you happy to see me?" he asked.

Tiara started to cry, "you don't know how much I missed you."

She gave him a kiss and that truly got his attention.

"Come show me. He took his wife by her waist and placed her on his lap. He grabbed her by her neck and gave her this long-awaited kiss.

Terrance missed his wife so much. He yearned for every part of her body. He slowly slid his hands underneath her nightgown. Tiara didn't have any underwear on. He moved up to her breast and cupped them gently. Tiara threw her head back, loving every touch that he was giving her. She finally took her nightgown off exposing her naked body. Terrance pause to look at her. He briefly admiried how beautiful she looked, her face just gave off this glow. He was feeling blessed to have her. Terrance took her breasts out and placed one into his mouth. He sucked and licked all over it. He then bit on each nipple. Terrance was getting aroused by this.

His manhood began to grow. Feeling this reaction Tiara got excited. She raised up off his lap a little, grabbed his dick and then inserted it inside of her. She was dripping wet by this time. They let out a sigh. They both were longing for this for two years. Tiara started to grind real slow raising her hips up and down. Terrance was enjoying every bit of it. He hoped that he wouldn't cum fast.

He grabbed her by her waist and began to grind back and forth with her. Tears came down Tiara's face. This was feeling so good to her. Her speed started to get faster.

"You missed this pussy Daddy?" she asked.

"You know I did T" he responded.

"Show me" she said.

Terrance flipped her around. Now she was laying on her back. He spread her legs wide and then proceeded to go deep inside of her.

Terrance felt like he was in heaven. Tiara's pussy was dripping wet and it was driving him crazy.

Tiara was in rhythm with his motion. Her inside walls started to jump around his dick.

"Yes, baby I feel you. Grab on this dick" Terrance instructed.

Tiara was out of control.

"Baby I can't hold it. I wanna cum" she yelled out.

"Cum for Daddy, Baby, let me feel it on my dick" Terrance whispered in her ear.

He started fucking her harder and harder until she exploded all over him.

"Yesss, Baby, that's just what I like" he said.

Tiara felt drained but she wasn't finished. She pushed Terrance off her and turned him around. With no warning she shoved his entire dick in her mouth. Sucking her juices off him.

Terrance couldn't take it. He took her by her hair and began to fuck her mouth. Tiara was sucking away and pinching on his nipples at the same time. Terrance was trying to control himself but couldn't. He released all his juices into Tiara's mouth. Tiara swallowed every drop and continued sucking without skipping a beat. Terrance was still nice and hard. He told her to get on her knees. Tiara did as she was told.

Once on her knees, she arched her back. All you saw was her nice round ass in the air. Terrance gave it a slap.

Slap!

"Do it again baby" she requested.

Terrance did it a couple of times before he started fucking her again.

Slap! Slap! Slap!

He slid right back in that wet spot. At first, he was sliding in and out real slow. Rubbing on her ass with his eyes closed. Thinking to himself how many nights he wished for this. How many nights he missed her touch, and her kisses. He had missed her, period. He spread open her ass cheeks and picked up the speed of his thrust. He started watching his dick go in and out. All Tiara's juices were all over him.

"This feel sooo good, I don't want to stop baby," he said.

"You don't have to Daddy," she moaned.

"Damn, why this pussy so wet?" he asked.

"You made it like that. You been missing this Baby?" She asked.

"You know I did."

"Show me, I want you to cum Daddy. Pleaseeee" she begged.

Tiara started throwing her ass back on Terrance's dick. Terrance was going harder and harder. Tiara spread her legs wider and began to play with herself while he was inside of her. Tiara knew Terrance loved when she did that. "Come on baby, cum with me," she demanded. "Terrance's whole body started to shiver. He was trying to control it, but he couldn't. Once again, he let off a load. He collapsed onto Tiara's back out of breath. He wrapped his arms around her and laid in silence for a while. This was the best feeling Tiara had felt in a while. She had her husband back home finally. Terrance was still trying to get himself together, when Tiara turned around and said,

"Baby, you ready for round three?"

THE END

Author
C.L Hawkins

"You must truly know my struggles
to appreciate my accomplishments."

CPSIA information can be obtained
at www.ICGtesting.com
Printed in the USA
BVHW031940240821
615149BV00008B/79

9 781795 524704